A POET'S JOURNAL Exploring Nature and the Seasons

poems about nature

Compiled by Joanne Randolph

Published in 2018 by The Rosen Publishing Group, Inc.
29 East 21st Street, New York, NY 10010

Credits:
"Seasons" by Leni Marshall, art by Kathy Couri, *Babybug* Magazine January 2014
"Mole Cricket" by Sandra Liatsos, art by Carolyn Digby Conahan, *Cricket* Magazine July 2006
"Our Garden" by Asia Porter, art by Gavin Rowe, *Babybug* Magazine May 2011
"Roly-Poly" by Caren Salas, art by Jaime Zollars, *Ladybug* Magazine June 2014
"The Little Stream" by Dale Cross Purvis, art by Margie Moore, *Babybug* Magazine May 2012
"Celebration" by Marion Dane Bauer, art by Christiane Krömer, *Cricket* Magazine October 2006
"In the Barn" by Candace Pearson, art by Kristina Swarner, *Cricket* Magazine November 2015
"Life of a Leaf" by Buffy Silverman, art by Shelly Hehenberger, *Cricket* Magazine October 2016
"All You Need" by Howard Schwartz, art by Kristina Swarner, *Cricket* Magazine November 2016
"Enjoy the Earth" Traditional Yoruba Chant, art by Joani Rothernberg, *Ladybug* Magazine March 2007
"Fruit Riddles" by Mary Quattlebaum, art by Jeffrey Ebbeler, *Ladybug* Magazine June 2011
"Buzz" by Maribeth Hamilton, art by Irene Haas, *Ladybug* Magazine June 2007
"The Secret Seed" by Allan Wolf, art by Peggy Collins, *Ladybug* Magazine May 2009
"Nature's Treasures" by Jane Morris Udovic, art by Jill Dubin, *Ladybug* Magazine June 2009
"A Country Road" by Grace Cornell Tall, art by Emma Shaw-Smith, *Ladybug* Magazine March 2010
"Pumpkin Seeds" by Aria Smith, art by Dorothy Stott, *Ladybug* Magazine, October 2011
"Which Part Do We Eat?" by Katherine Ayres, art by Carolyn Croll, *Ladybug* Magazine June 2011
"Solstice" by Caroline Starr Rose, art by Lauren Lowen, *Spider* Magazine November 2016
"Backyard Acrobat" by Laura Sassi, art by Lauren Pettapiece, *Spider* Magazine January 2007

Book Design: Tanya Dellaccio
Editor: Joanne Randolph

Cataloging-in-Publication Data
Names: Randolph, Joanne.
Title: Poems about nature / compiled by Joanne Randolph.
Description: New York : Windmill Books, 2018. | Series: A poet's journal: exploring nature and the seasons | Includes index.
Identifiers: LCCN ISBN 9781508197027 (pbk.) | ISBN 9781508197010 (library bound) | ISBN 9781508197034 (6 pack)
Subjects: LCSH: Nature–Juvenile poetry. | Children's poetry, American.
Classification: LCC PS595.N22 P64 2018 | DDC [E]–dc23

Manufactured in the United States of America

CPSIA Compliance Information: Batch #BS18WM: For Further Information contact Rosen Publishing, New York, New York at 1-800-237-9932

CONTENTS

SEASONS

by: Leni Marshall
art by: Kathy Couri

Hats and mittens, boots with strings,
cozy coats are winter things.
Swimsuits, sandals, and sunglasses
will come out when winter passes!

MOLE CRICKET

by: Sandra Liatsos
art by: Carolyn Digby Conahan

His legs in front
are shovels digging
tunnels underground.
His legs in back
are paddles pushing
piles of dirt around.
He hollows rooms
throughout his house
and rubs his wings to sing;
his tunnels
amplify the sound
to crickets
up above the ground
who hear the music king.

OUR GARDEN

by: Asia Porter
art by: Gavin Rowe

Digging, raking, sowing,
Weeding, watering, hoeing...
Look! Our garden's growing.

ROLY-POLY

by: Caren Salas
art by: Jaime Zollars

Teeny, tiny Roly-Poly,
Down upon the ground you crawl.
Can you tell me, will you show me,
How you roll up like a ball?
Can you roll up like a Roly-Poly?

THE LITTLE STREAM

by Dale Cross Purvis
art by: Margie Moore

The little stream ripples
As it rushes along,
While everyone hushes
To hear its sweet song,
A *jing-a-ling, ting-a-ling*
Tune that it knows
And sings to the children
Wherever it goes.

CELEBRATION

by: Marion Dane Bauer
art by: Christiane Krömer

Willow with hair freshly washed
is always first to arrive
at the Spring party.

When Autumn comes
and oak and maple
have shouted their loud goodbyes,
when birch has tossed down
the last golden coins,
pale willow still
stays,
whispering,
whispering.

IN THE BARN

by: Candace Pearson
art by: Kristina Swarner

Something's coming
this cold, dark night.
We gather in the barn by lantern light.
Lying on the straw
our chestnut mare
whinnies as I whisper,
"Don't be scared."

Something's coming,
it won't be long.
In the eaves, dove
coos a rockabye song.
Here it comes–
all slick-wet hair
and wobbly legged–
a chestnut heir!

LIFE OF A LEAF

by: Buffy Silverman
art by: Shelly Hehenberger

A
leaf
is a map with
roadways of sap,
its food-making
factories
shipping out
calories,
feeding and ferrying,
breathing and carrying,
soaking up sunshine
till fall's final deadline,
then changes its
clothes for a
colorful
s
h
o
w

ALL YOU NEED

by: Howard Schwartz
art by: Kristina Swarner

You need
a planet
to live on,

a sun
to give you light
and warmth,

clouds
to gather rain,

seeds
to take root,

trees
to create air
for you to breathe.

You need a land
in which you are welcome,

and someone
to watch over you.

You need words
to share your thoughts,

a hand
to write those words down,

a beating heart.

ENJOY THE EARTH

Traditional Yoruba Chant
art by: Joani Rothenberg

Enjoy the earth gently
Enjoy the earth gently
For if the earth is spoiled
It cannot be repaired
Enjoy the earth gently

FRUIT RIDDLES

by: Mary Quattlebaum
art by: Jeffrey Ebbeler

What's purple or green
and good for lunch?
You can nibble one
or eat a bunch.

What's yellow outside
and white within?
What's curved like the moon
or a big, bright grin?

What's green and sweet
in a brown, hairy suit?
Can you believe
this thing is a fruit?

BUZZ

by: Maribeth Hamilton
art by: Irene Haas

Be very still. Don't move an inch.
Don't wiggle or giggle or jiggle or flinch.

This wee little bee is just taking a rest.
Soon she'll be off on another quest,

Floating and flitting to and fro,
Spreading pollen so flowers will grow.

THE SECRET SEED

by: Allan Wolf
art by: Peggy Collins

A seed holds tomorrow
inside her shell.
What will she be?
She will not tell.

To find out what,
you'll have to wait
and watch her grow
from grain to great.

Each gardener is planting some seeds.
What kinds of seeds have they planted?

NATURE'S TREASURES

by: Jane Morris Udovic
art by: Jill Dubin

I know by heart the shapes of leaves,
the smell of dirt, the buzz of bees.
And when it rains I hear each drop
and count them all until they stop.
I know how ants move in a line
and where to pet a porcupine.
I imitate the songs of birds
and love to hear their chirpy words.
I know how pussy willows feel
and what a tree trunk's rings reveal.
As I explore the earth each day
for hidden treasures tucked away,
I wonder what the world can see
when it sits back and looks at me.

A COUNTRY ROAD

by: Grace Cornell Tall
art by: Emma Shaw-Smith

Traffic is never dull or still
On the country road
That climbs my hill.
A dawdling crow and a dusty toad
Are likely travelers on this road.
A tardy rabbit hurrying home,
And a garden snake with an urge to roam
Add to the crowd, and if you please,
There's quite a bustle of bugs and bees,
A dragonfly, a traveling mouse,
And an old box turtle relocating his house
Are some of the things that you might see
If you should decide to visit me.

PUMPKIN SEEDS

by: Aria Smith
art by: Dorothy Stott

A duck in the reeds found some pumpkin
seeds.
A stout pink pig found a place to dig.
A furry brown mole dug a great big hole.
A little black ant came to help them plant.
A dark gray cloud brought lots of rain,
And then the sun came out again.
The seeds reached down with new white roots.
The seeds reached up with bright green shoots.
The leaves did grow, the vines did climb,
Until October—harvesttime!
Then Ant and Moley danced a jig
While Duck baked pumpkins with the pig.
They all sat down to pumpkin pie,
Which they ate by the reeds when the moon
was high.

WHICH PART DO WE EAT?

by: Katherine Ayres
art by: Carolyn Croll

Let's run to the garden and pick us a treat!
But . . . which part do we eat?

Green beans, okras,
and peppers are odd . . .
We eat the pod.

Tomatoes and baby
zucchini are cute . . .
We eat the fruit.

Asparagus, celery?
What about them?
We eat the stem.
Lettuce, spinach, and chard?
I believe . . .
We eat the leaves.
Carrots and turnips
and yams aren't fruit . . .
We eat the root.

Peas, corn, and lima beans
aren't weeds . . .
We eat the seeds.
Broccoli's filled
with vitamin power . . .
We eat the flower.
Stem, leaf, pod, fruit,
Flower, seed, or sturdy root–

Chop them and cook them and serve them on dishes.
Fresh crispy veggies are mighty delicious!

SOLSTICE

by: Caroline Starr Rose
art by: Lauren Lowen

Welcome, winter,
longest night,
frozen mornings,
day's short light.

Hello, summer,
sun runs long,
golden evenings,
night's brief song.

BACKYARD ACROBAT

by: Laura Sassi
art by: Lauren Pettapiece

I made the birds a tasty treat
With bagel, seeds, and string
And peanut butter thickly spread
To make the birdseeds cling.
But before the backyard birds could sup
Upon this wintry feast,
From far below came darting up
A different kind of beast.
He nimbly balanced on a branch
And stuffed his cheeks with seeds,
Then swinging like an acrobat
He ate the whole trapeze!
And when he'd finally had his fill
Of my sticky birdseed ring,
He scurried back from whence he came,
Leaving only crumbs and string.

QUESTIONS TO THINK ABOUT

In your head or on a separate piece of paper, answer the following questions:

These poems talk about different things in nature, from plants and animals, to weather and seasons. The poets use different devices to paint a picture for the reader. Can you find an example of onomatopoeia? How about alliteration?

Some of these poems give us real science information. Take a look at the poems about seeds and growing gardens. What do you need to make plants grow?

What are some of the qualities of nature, according to these poems?

According to these poems, what are some of the animals and insects you might see in nature?

INDEX